LOVE IS THE BRIDGE
Mood of America
Series

Lunch Box
Reflective Storybook
Therapy
Quick Relief Magnet

An American Journey
Through Fire and Hope

Love is the Bridge

Arthur McMillian's story can be found in four formats:

**Novella - Amazon Store
**Coloring Book - Amazon Store
**Audio - Audible Book Store
**Journal- Amazon Store

MOOD IN AMERICA SERIES

A Reflective Journey Through Words, Pages, and Color – 2025 and Beyond

Puzzle Books *for the Mind*

MOOD *in* AMERICA COLORING BOOK

CURRENT EVENTS 2025

Guided Journals *for the Heart*

LOVE IS *the* BRIDGE

AN AMERICAN REFLECTIVE JOURNEY THROUGH FIRE *and* HOPE

Coloring Books *for the Soul*

Other Works - Amazon

Available Now on Amazon – Collect the Complete Series

An American Journey Through Fire and Hope

LOVE IS THE BRIDGE

An American Journey Through Fire and Hope
A Novella

Copyright

ISBN (Paperback): 978-1-58401-050-0
ISBN (EBook): 978-58401-051-7
Printed in the United States of America

An American Journey Through Fire and Hope

Love is the Bridge

Dedication

For those who chose love when hate was easier,
and for the hands that built bridges so others could cross.

To my beloved husband of 55 years, affectionately known as Papa Brown, age 78, and to his treasured friends at Mike's service station, especially Mike, my adopted son, and Kenneth, who fills my house with beautiful treasures.

To my extraordinary grandson Raphael Chino, may this story ignite a spark within you that inspires you throughout your life.

And to all the remarkable children I have had the privilege to teach: I hope I have imparted my spirit, actions, and words in ways that uplift and empower you. Every moment I spent with you has been a joy, and each of you has profoundly influenced my life..

An American Journey Through Fire and Hope

Epigraph

Hate builds walls; love builds bridges.
Hatred is heavy; love is light.

Author's Note

America's story is complicated—scarred and shining, fractured and resilient. This novella is a fictional account drawn from the atmosphere of the Civil Rights era through today, seen through the life of Arthur McMillian. While Arthur is not a historical figure, his journey is stitched from threads that many have lived: loss and courage, injustice and hope, anger and forgiveness.

I wrote this book to honor the quiet heroes—teachers who risked their standing to nurture minds, nurses who cared even when met with suspicion, neighbors who stepped into harm's way, elders who carried wisdom across generations, and young people who keep choosing bridges over walls.

If you find yourself in these pages—if you've ever felt unseen, unheard, or unwelcome—this story is for you. May it remind you that love is not a feeling we wait for; it is a practice we live. It is the hardest work, and the holiest.

Thank you for reading with an open heart.

— Mrs. Brown, The Encourager, 2025

An American Journey Through Fire and Hope

Love is the Bridge

Part One

Table of Contents

An American Journey Through Fire and Hope

Born in the Fire

Chapter One --- Born in the Fire

Birmingham, Alabama, 1955.

The summer air was thick with heat and smoke, the kind that clung to your lungs and made the world feel heavy. For six-year-old Arthur McMillian, the world was already heavy. His father, a factory worker, had been taken from him just months earlier—an accident, they said, though his mother often muttered about broken machines and corners cut.

He remembered the day of the funeral, the way his mother's hand gripped his so tightly it hurt. She wore her best blue dress, the one she saved for church, and her eyes seemed fixed somewhere far beyond the preacher's words. Arthur didn't cry then; he didn't quite understand loss. But when he walked home past the factory gates, saw the smoke rising from the same chimneys that had swallowed his father, he understood enough to feel afraid.

Life in Birmingham was divided down the middle, and Arthur was born on the wrong side of the line. He saw it everywhere: the "Whites Only" sign above the drinking

An American Journey Through Fire and Hope

Love is the Bridge

fountain at the drugstore, the seats they couldn't sit in on the bus, the school that stood across town with shining windows and new books, while his own classroom was patched together with scraps.

One afternoon, walking home from school, he tugged at his mother's sleeve.

"Why can't I drink from that fountain?" he asked, pointing at the one marked with polished letters: Whites Only.

His mother crouched to meet his eyes. Her face was tired, her hands worn, but her voice was steady.

"Because some folks don't see us for what we are, Arthur," she said softly. "But you must always see yourself. Do you hear me? Always."

That night, lying on his thin mattress, Arthur

An American Journey Through Fire and Hope

Love is the Bridge

whispered those words over and over like a prayer. Always see yourself.

The world outside was burning. The city was a flashpoint, a place where the fight for justice had already taken root. He could hear the marches sometimes—voices rising together like thunder rolling down the streets. His uncle called them troublemakers. His mother called them brave.

Arthur didn't know what he thought yet. All he knew was that when he closed his eyes, he could see two worlds: one where he stayed silent and small, and one where he stood tall, even when the fire raged around him.

And even at six years old, Arthur McMillian felt the pull of that second world.

Love is the Bridge

See each other
Listen with love
Share Burdens
Forgive but not forget
Build bridges, not walls
Live hope Daily

LOVE
...suffereth long

An American Journey
Through Fire and Hope

The World Shakes

✳ Chapter Two – The World Shakes

By the time Arthur turned ten, Birmingham was no longer just smoke and sweat from the factories — it was fire hoses and police dogs, shouts that split the air, and songs that carried hope through the streets.

He didn't need to read a newspaper to know his city was on edge. He saw it in the eyes of the men who gathered on porches at night, whispering. He felt it in the way his mother locked the doors tighter when the marches passed their block.

One Sunday, after church, his older cousin grabbed his hand. "Come on, Arthur. You need to see this."

Arthur held those words like a shield. But even at ten, he knew that overcoming wouldn't be easy.

They slipped into the crowd forming downtown. The marchers were dressed in their best clothes, holding hands, singing as they walked.

The sound was soft but powerful, a river of voices

The World Shakes

winding through the city.

But waiting for them were men in uniforms, their faces hard, their clubs in hand.

Arthur's cousin pulled him behind a lamppost as the first clash began. Water from the hoses roared like thunder, knocking women to the ground. Dogs snapped and barked, their handlers shoving them forward. People screamed, but the marchers—many of them just teenagers—kept singing through their fear.

Arthur gripped the pole so tightly his palms hurt. His chest shook. He wanted to run, but something inside him told him not to look away. He had to see. He had to remember.

That night, lying awake, he whispered to his mother, "Why do they hate us so much?"

She brushed his hair back and kissed his

forehead.

"They're afraid, baby. Afraid of losing the power they never should have had. But fear can't win forever."

Weeks later, his church bused members to Montgomery to hear Dr. King speak. Arthur sat on his mother's lap, peering over heads. He couldn't remember all the words, but he remembered the voice — strong, rolling like waves, carrying more than hope. It carried certainty.

We shall overcome.

Love is the Bridge

- See each other
- Listen with love
- Share Burdens
- Forgive but not forget
- Build bridges, not walls
- Live hope Daily

LOVE
...is kind

An American Journey Through Fire and Hope

A Teacher's Secret

❄ Chapter Three – A Teacher's Secret

The school Arthur attended was old, its paint peeling, its books hand-me-downs from the white school across town. The covers were torn, the pages scribbled with names that weren't his. But he read them anyway. He loved words, how they could carry him beyond the fences and signs that hemmed him in.

Mrs. Parker, his teacher, noticed. She was white, young, and not from Birmingham. Most white teachers didn't last long in a Black school, but she stayed. She had a quiet way about her, strict but kind, and when Arthur read aloud, she always gave him a smile that felt like sunlight.

One afternoon, after class, she asked him to stay behind.

"Arthur, do you like books?" she asked.

"Yes, ma'am."

A Teacher's Secret

"Do you want harder ones?"

He nodded, though he wasn't sure if she meant "harder" as in "challenging" or "dangerous."

She pulled a worn copy of To Kill a Mockingbird from her bag. "This isn't on our list," she whispered, glancing toward the hallway. "But I think you'll like it. Just... don't tell anyone I gave it to you."

Arthur took the book, his fingers trembling.

From then on, every week, Mrs. Parker slipped him another book. History, poetry, novels — words he devoured late at night by lamplight, careful to keep the covers hidden.

One evening, his mother found him with the book open across his knees.

"Where did you get that?" she asked, suspicion

Love is the Bridge

A Teacher's Secret

in her voice.

"Mrs. Parker gave it to me."

His mother frowned, then sighed. "Be careful, baby. Some folks don't like it when we know too much."

But she didn't take the book away.

Years later, Arthur would realize how much risk Mrs. Parker had taken. A white teacher helping a Black boy succeed could have cost her more than her job in Birmingham. But she did it anyway.

On his last day in her class, she bent down, handed him one final book, and whispered: "Your mind is too bright to be dimmed by hate. Don't ever let them tell you otherwise."

Arthur carried that line with him for the rest of his life.

An American Journey Through Fire and Hope

Love is the Bridge

See each other
Listen with love
Share Burdens
Forgive but not forget
Build bridges, not walls
Live hope Daily

LOVE
...endureth all things

An American Journey Through Fire and Hope

❄ Chapter Four – A Vow of Dignity

April 1968.

Arthur was thirteen when the news broke. He was sitting at the dinner table, eating beans and cornbread, when the radio crackled with the voice that made his mother drop her fork.

"Dr. Martin Luther King Jr. has been shot... in Memphis..."

The rest blurred. His mother pressed her hands to her face and sobbed, the sound tearing through the small house like a storm.

Arthur's chest tightened. He had heard King's voice just two years before, had felt the power in his words. Now that voice was gone, silenced by a bullet.

Love is the Bridge

A Vow of Dignity

That night, the city erupted. People poured into the streets, shouting, crying, some throwing rocks, some setting fires. The grief was too big, too heavy to hold quietly.

Arthur slipped outside and stood on the porch, watching the smoke rise. His cousin ran by, urging him to join. "We gotta show them we won't take this no more!"

But something inside Arthur held him still. He remembered the marches, the songs, the way people had stood tall even when the hoses knocked them down. He remembered King's words: "Darkness cannot drive out darkness. Only light can do that."

He whispered those words like a shield.

His mother came to the door, eyes red, voice trembling. "Don't you go out there, Arthur. Don't you give hate your hands."

An American Journey Through Fire and Hope

Love is the Bridge

A Vow of Dignity

He nodded, though his heart ached with a fire he didn't know how to put out.

That night, lying awake, he stared at the ceiling and made himself a promise:

I will not let hate make me its servant. I will fight, but I will fight with dignity. I will fight with love.

The vow settled into him like a seed, fragile but alive.

An American Journey
Through Fire and Hope

Love is the Bridge

- See each other
- Listen with love
- Share Burdens
- Forgive but not forget
- Build bridges, not walls
- Live hope Daily

LOVE

...hopeth all things

An American Journey Through Fire and Hope

❄ Chapter Five – The College Dream

By 1973, Arthur was eighteen, tall, serious-eyed, and hungry for more than Birmingham's broken streets could give him. He wanted education. He wanted a future.

His mother had worked two jobs, ironing clothes by day and scrubbing offices by night, to save what little she could. When the acceptance letter arrived — Alabama State University, a historically Black college — she held it to her chest and wept.

"You're the first, Arthur," she whispered. "The first in our family to walk this road. Don't forget who you carry with you."

Campus life was alive with possibilities, but prejudice still walked its halls. Arthur sat in classrooms with outdated books, overhearing

Love is the Bridge

The College Dream

whispers about how "boys like him" didn't belong in certain careers.

When he applied for a part-time job at the library, the manager laughed. "You're strong — go work in maintenance."

The sting lingered, but Arthur swallowed his pride and found work in the cafeteria instead. Nights, he studied history until his eyes burned, determined to understand not just his story, but the story of his people.

History became his compass. He poured over stories of Frederick Douglass, Harriet Tubman, and W.E.B. Du Bois. He scribbled notes in the margins: They endured. So must I.

He also found joy. He met Lillian, a bright-eyed nursing student with a laugh like sunlight. They studied together, walked hand in hand across

An American Journey Through Fire and Hope

Love is the Bridge

The College Dream

campus, and dreamed aloud about futures that seemed just barely possible.

But the world outside still pressed its weight against him. Police stopped him twice while driving to campus — once accusing him of stealing his own car, once forcing him to sit on the curb while they searched his books for drugs.

Each time, he thought of his vow: I will not let hate make me its servant.

When graduation came in 1977, Arthur stood in cap and gown, his mother in the crowd wiping tears from her cheeks. He looked out at her, at Lillian beside her, and felt the weight of generations.

He was the first to walk the stage. But he swore he would not be the last.

An American Journey Through Fire and Hope

Love is the Bridge

- See each other
- Listen with love
- Share Burdens
- Forgive but not forget
- Build bridges, not walls
- Live hope Daily

LOVE
...beareth all things

An American Journey
Through Fire and Hope

❄ Chapter Six – Building and Breaking

By 1980, Arthur McMillian was a married man. He and Lillian wed in the small Baptist church where he'd once sung in the children's choir. The sanctuary was filled with neighbors, cousins, and friends, and as they walked down the aisle, Arthur felt like he was carrying more than just his own dreams. He was carrying a whole people's prayer: that love could last, that life could be built, even in hard soil.

They rented a small house on the east side of Montgomery. It wasn't much — creaky floors, peeling paint — but it was theirs. Within two years, the walls rang with the cries and laughter of two children, Marcus and Renee.

Arthur worked as a history teacher at a local high school. He loved the classroom. He loved showing his students the lives of leaders who had carved paths where none existed. But the

Building and Breaking

job came with its own walls. Promotions passed him by, always going to younger white teachers with less experience.

At parent meetings, he was sometimes mistaken for the janitor. Once, a colleague suggested he "tone down" his lectures on civil rights, as if history itself might make someone uncomfortable.

Lillian bore her own struggles as a nurse. Patients refused her care. Supervisors doubted her skill. Yet she returned home each night with a smile, telling Arthur, "They can't take away my compassion. That belongs to me."

Their marriage was strong, but the world tested them. In 1987, Arthur applied for a city grant to fund an after-school history program. It was denied without explanation. Later, he overheard a councilman laugh:

Love is the Bridge

Building and Breaking

"Why would we fund something that just stirs up old wounds?"

That night, he sat at the kitchen table, staring at the rejection letter. Lillian laid her hand over his.

"You're planting seeds, Arthur. Just because they don't water them doesn't mean they won't grow."

He nodded, though a quiet bitterness gnawed at him.

He wanted so much more for his children. He wanted doors open that had been slammed in his face.

Still, each morning, he rose before dawn, kissed Lillian's forehead, and whispered to himself the vow he had made as a boy: I will not let hate make me its servant.

An American Journey Through Fire and Hope

Love is the Bridge

He was building a life. But in every brick he laid, there were cracks — cracks carved by a world that refused to see him fully.

LOVE IS THE BRIDGE

An American Journey Through Fire and Hope

Love is the Bridge

Part Two

Table of Contents

An American Journey Through Fire and Hope

❄ Chapter Seven – Violence and Grace

The summer of 1992 was heavy with heat and tension. Across the nation, the news carried images of protests, of cities on edge after yet another act of police brutality. In Montgomery, anger simmered under the surface — not always visible, but always present, like a crack beneath the pavement waiting to split.

Arthur was driving home one evening after a long day at school. He had stayed late, grading papers and preparing for the fall semester. The streets were quiet, the sky painted with streaks of orange and purple. He rolled down his window to feel the air, humming a hymn his grandmother used to sing.

That's when the headlights flared in his rearview mirror.

A truck pulled up close, too close, its horn

Violence and Grace

blaring. Before he could react, it swerved ahead, blocking his path. Three men jumped out — young, white, their voices sharp with curses.

"Get outta the car, boy!"

The word boy stung more than the fists that followed. They dragged him from the seat, slammed him against the hood, and began to beat him. Punches to his ribs, kicks to his legs, a boot pressing down on his neck.

Arthur's mind screamed, Fight back! His hands clenched, his vow trembling on the edge of breaking. But as blood filled his mouth, he heard his grandmother's voice: "Hatred is heavy. Love is lighter to carry."

Something shifted inside him. He went limp, not in surrender, but in defiance. He refused to give them what they wanted — his rage.

Love is the Bridge

Violence and Grace

Neighbors spilled into the street, shouting, calling the police. The attackers fled, leaving him broken on the pavement.

Lillian rushed to the hospital, her hands trembling as she touched his battered face.

"Why didn't you fight back?" she whispered through tears.

Arthur, barely able to speak, rasped: "Because then they'd have won twice."

The next week, bruises still blooming across his skin, Arthur stood before his church. The sanctuary was packed, anger burning in every pew. People expected fury, demands for vengeance.

Instead, he spoke with a quiet strength.

"I forgive them," he said. The room fell silent. "Not

An American Journey Through Fire and Hope

Love is the Bridge

Violence and Grace

because they deserve it. But because I refuse to let their hate live in me."

Gasps. Murmurs. Some shook their heads, unable to understand. Others wept.

Forgiveness did not erase the pain. It did not heal his ribs or his pride overnight. But it broke the chain that threatened to bind him to bitterness.

In that moment, Arthur McMillian became something more than a teacher, more than a victim. He became a bridge.

**LOVE IS THE BRIDGE.
TOGETHER, WE
CARRY IT FORWARD.**

An American Journey Through Fire and Hope

The Weight of Love

✳ Chapter Eight – The Weight of Love

Winter of 1994 came cold and sharp. The trees stood bare, and the streets of Birmingham seemed quieter, as if the city itself was holding its breath. For Arthur, the silence carried a deeper weight — his grandmother, the woman who had held the family together with prayer and wisdom, had grown frail.

She was the one who rocked him to sleep when his father died, who pressed Scripture into his hands before he could even read. She had always told him, "Child, life will hand you stones. Don't you carry them all. Lay them down at the Lord's feet, or they'll crush you."

Now, as she lay in a narrow bed, her breath thin and uneven, Arthur sat beside her, holding her hand.

Love is the Bridge

"Grandma," he whispered, his throat tight, "I don't know if I can keep doing this. Teaching, forgiving, carrying so much. It's heavy."

Her lips cracked into the faintest smile. "Hatred, baby... hatred is the heaviest load of all. Love is lighter. Carry that instead."

Tears stung his eyes. He wanted to ask how. How could he carry love in a world that kept spitting back hate? But her eyes closed before he could speak.

Her funeral drew neighbors, church members, and family from miles away. They filled the pews, singing hymns she had loved, voices cracking under the weight of loss.

Arthur spoke at the service, his voice trembling.

An American Journey Through Fire and Hope

Love is the Bridge

The Weight of Love

"She taught me that love isn't soft. Love is strength. Love is what keeps us standing when hate tries to knock us down. And if I have anything worth giving to my children, my students, my community... it's that lesson."

Afterward, he walked home slowly, snow crunching under his shoes. He carried no Bible, no speech, only her words, burning into his heart like scripture of their own:

Hatred is heavy. Love is lighter to carry.

From that day forward, he would not only repeat those words. He would live them.

An American Journey Through Fire and Hope

Love is the Bridge

See each other
Listen with love
Share Burdens
Forgive but not forget
Build bridges, not walls
Live hope Daily

LOVE ..believeth all things

An American Journey Through Fire and Hope

※ Chapter Nine – A Nation in Flux

The year 2001 dawned with promise. Arthur was in his mid-forties, his children nearly grown, and the house that once echoed with diapers and lullabies now hummed with college applications and restless dreams. Marcus wanted to study law; Renee dreamed of becoming a doctor. Arthur and Lillian beamed with pride.

But that September morning changed everything.

He was in his classroom when the whispers spread, when televisions flickered on, and students watched the towers fall in New York.. Gasps, tears, silence.

For weeks after, the country seemed to draw together in grief, strangers holding hands, churches overflowing, flags waving on every porch.

Yet beneath the unity, Arthur felt the old cracks widening. He saw Muslim neighbors harassed, students teased for their faith, and airports full of suspicion. He remembered the fear of his own childhood, the way hate could disguise itself as "safety."

Love is the Bridge

At night, he and Lillian would sit on the porch, listening to the news. She shook her head. "Seems like every time we come together, fear comes knocking again."

He nodded, his heart heavy. "It's like the soil ain't never settled. Storms keep stirring it up."

Still, he kept teaching. He told his students the story of his grandmother, of the vow he made as a boy, of the beating he endured and the forgiveness he chose. At first, they listened politely. But slowly, Arthur saw their eyes light with recognition. Some began calling him Mr. Bridge Builder.

By 2008, when America elected its first Black president, Arthur wept openly. He gathered Marcus and Renee in his arms and whispered, "Your grandfather couldn't vote. I was chased for trying. But look now... look at what's possible."

But with pride came backlash. He heard the whispers in town, saw the venom in certain headlines. Fear and resentment boiled again,

An American Journey Through Fire and Hope

Love is the Bridge

A Nation in Flux

louder, sharper.

Through it all, Arthur stood steady. He spoke at schools, churches, even city meetings. He told anyone who would listen: "Hate is a wall. Love is a bridge."

Some dismissed him as naïve. Others told him he was too soft, too forgiving. But he knew better. He had carried hate's weight before. He refused to carry it again.

The nation was in flux. Unity one day, division the next. But Arthur believed in seeds — seeds of truth, compassion, courage. Seeds he could plant in his students, his children, his neighbors.

The storms might rage. But storms also watered the soil.

And Arthur McMillian had learned long ago: with enough faith, seeds can grow in even the hardest ground.

An American Journey Through Fire and Hope

Love is the Bridge

See each other
Listen with love
Share Burdens
Forgive but not forget
Build bridges, not walls
Live hope Daily

LOVE
...does not seek her own

An American Journey
Through Fire and Hope

✳ Chapter Ten – Joy and Sorrow

By the mid-2010s, Arthur's pride swelled each time he looked at his children. Marcus had become a lawyer, arguing cases for those who couldn't afford strong voices. Renee wore her white coat with grace, healing bodies in a hospital where her mother once struggled for respect.

At family dinners, they laughed, teased each other, and filled the little house with life. Arthur often leaned back, watching them, feeling like the sacrifices of generations were blooming before his eyes. This is what we fought for, he thought. This is the harvest.

But storms do not ask permission to enter a home.

It began with Lillian's cough — soft at first, then lingering, then sharp. Doctors ran tests, then came back with quiet eyes. Cancer. Advanced.

The word struck like lightning, splitting Arthur's world in two.

Love is the Bridge

Joy and Sorrow

He prayed. He begged. He carried her to treatments, sat through endless hospital hours, whispered to her at night when she couldn't sleep. Still, the disease spread like shadow through her body.

One evening, when the pain was sharpest, she took his hand. Her voice was weak, but her eyes shone steady.

"Arthur," she said, "don't let this make you bitter. You hear me? Promise me."

Tears streamed down his face. "I can't do this without you, Lil."

"Yes, you can," she whispered. "Because you'll carry love. That's lighter than grief."

Weeks later, in the stillness of a winter night, she slipped away, leaving only her warmth in his hand.

The house grew silent. Marcus and Renee checked in daily, but when they left, the nights swallowed him.

An American Journey
Through Fire and Hope

Love is the Bridge

Joy and Sorrow

He sat alone on the porch, staring at the stars, the weight of sorrow pressing on him heavier than any hatred he had ever faced.

He thought of his vow. He thought of his grandmother's words. But now, even love felt too heavy to lift.

One night, Marcus sat beside him. "Dad," he said, voice trembling, "Mom would want you to keep teaching, keep speaking."

Arthur shook his head. "What good are my words if I can't even save the one I love most?"

Silence. Then Renee, standing behind him, spoke softly: "Because your words saved us, Daddy. And we'll carry them now. For her. For you."

For the first time in months, Arthur wept openly, his children's arms around him. Grief would never leave him. But in their embrace, he felt the flicker of something he thought he'd lost forever.

An American Journey Through Fire and Hope

Love is the Bridge

Joy and Sorrow

Love had not died with Lillian. It was still alive — in Marcus's fire, in Renee's compassion, in the children they might one day raise.

And if love lived in them, perhaps he could find the strength to live it, too.

✳ Chapter Eleven – The Spark Returns

Grief is a shadow that lingers, even when the sun rises. For months after Lillian's death, Arthur lived in a fog. He went through the motions — teaching his classes and answering his children's calls — but his spirit felt hollow. The vow he made as a boy seemed far away, its fire dimmed.

Then one autumn afternoon in 2016, he walked past the courthouse downtown and heard voices. Loud, urgent, passionate. A group of young people held signs high, chanting for justice after yet another unarmed Black man had been killed.

Arthur stopped. He stood at the edge of the crowd, leaning on his cane now, his hair graying at the temples. He watched the fire in their eyes, the same fire he'd seen in the marches of his youth.

For the first time in months, something stirred inside him.

One of the organizers noticed him standing alone and walked over.

An American Journey
Through Fire and Hope

Love is the Bridge

The Spark Returns

"Sir," she said, "would you like to say something?"

Arthur shook his head. "I'm just passing by."

But she tilted her head. "No one just passes by justice."

Her words landed deep. And before he knew it, he was standing before the crowd, microphone trembling in his hand.

"I've seen this before," he began, his voice rough with age and grief. "In the sixties, we were knocked down with hoses, bitten by dogs, cursed in the streets. And I'll tell you what — they thought fear would silence us. But it didn't. And it won't silence you."

The crowd cheered, voices rising.

"And when they come at you with hate," he continued, "you'll be tempted to give it back. Don't. Hate is a wall. Love is a bridge. Build bridges, my children. Build them stronger than the walls they throw at you."

An American Journey Through Fire and Hope

Love is the Bridge

The Spark Returns

The chants swelled again, and Arthur stepped back, tears streaking his cheeks. For the first time since losing Lillian, he felt alive, connected, purposeful.

From then on, he began meeting with young activists — in coffee shops, at libraries, in church basements. They called him Grandpa Arthur. He listened to their frustrations, their strategies, their dreams. And when they grew weary, he reminded them: "The fight is long, but love will carry you farther than hate ever could."

In mentoring them, Arthur discovered something he hadn't expected — healing.

Each time he shared his story, he felt Lillian's presence beside him. Each time a young person called him "Grandpa," he felt the roots of family extending beyond blood.

The spark had returned. Not as a firestorm, but as a steady flame — one that would burn in him until his final days.

An American Journey Through Fire and Hope

Love is the Bridge

See each other
Listen with love
Share Burdens
Forgive but not forget
Build bridges, not walls
Live hope Daily

LOVE
...is not easily provoked

An American Journey
Through Fire and Hope

Holding the Line

�֍ Chapter Twelve – Holding the Line

By the late 2010s, Arthur had become a fixture in his community. He no longer marched at the front — his knees were too stiff for that now — but when people gathered, they asked him to speak. They called him The Bridge Builder.

He spoke in schools, his voice steady as he told children about the Birmingham of his youth, about the fountains marked "Whites Only," about the night Dr. King was taken from the world.

He told them about the vow he made at thirteen, the beating he survived in '92, and the forgiveness that baffled even his attackers.

Some students listened with wide eyes. Others rolled theirs, muttering, "That was then. Things are different now."

But when news broke of another protest, another tragedy, they remembered his words. And some sought him out, asking quietly: "How do we hold on without hate eating us alive?"

At churches, he leaned on the pulpit, gray hair catching the light, voice filling the sanctuary: "Hate is a wall. Love is a bridge. And I tell you this: walls keep us trapped. Bridges carry us forward."

At city meetings, when tempers flared, he raised a hand. His presence alone seemed to calm the room. People said he had "gravity," though he preferred to think of it as the weight of years — scars, lessons, losses, all gathered into a kind of wisdom.

Still, not everyone welcomed him. Some mocked him as too soft. Others accused him of preaching patience while the world demanded urgency. He did not argue. He only said, "My patience is not passivity. It is persistence. Love is not weakness. It is the hardest thing in the world."

In private, the nights were still long. Lillian's absence

Love is the Bridge

Holding the Line

was a hollow that never fully closed. But each time he spoke, each time a child called him Grandpa Arthur or a stranger pressed his hand in thanks, he felt her there — her compassion still alive in him.

The world was a stormy, divided, and often cruel place. But Arthur McMillian had chosen his vow long ago. And now, in his twilight years, he held the line — not with fists, but with love.

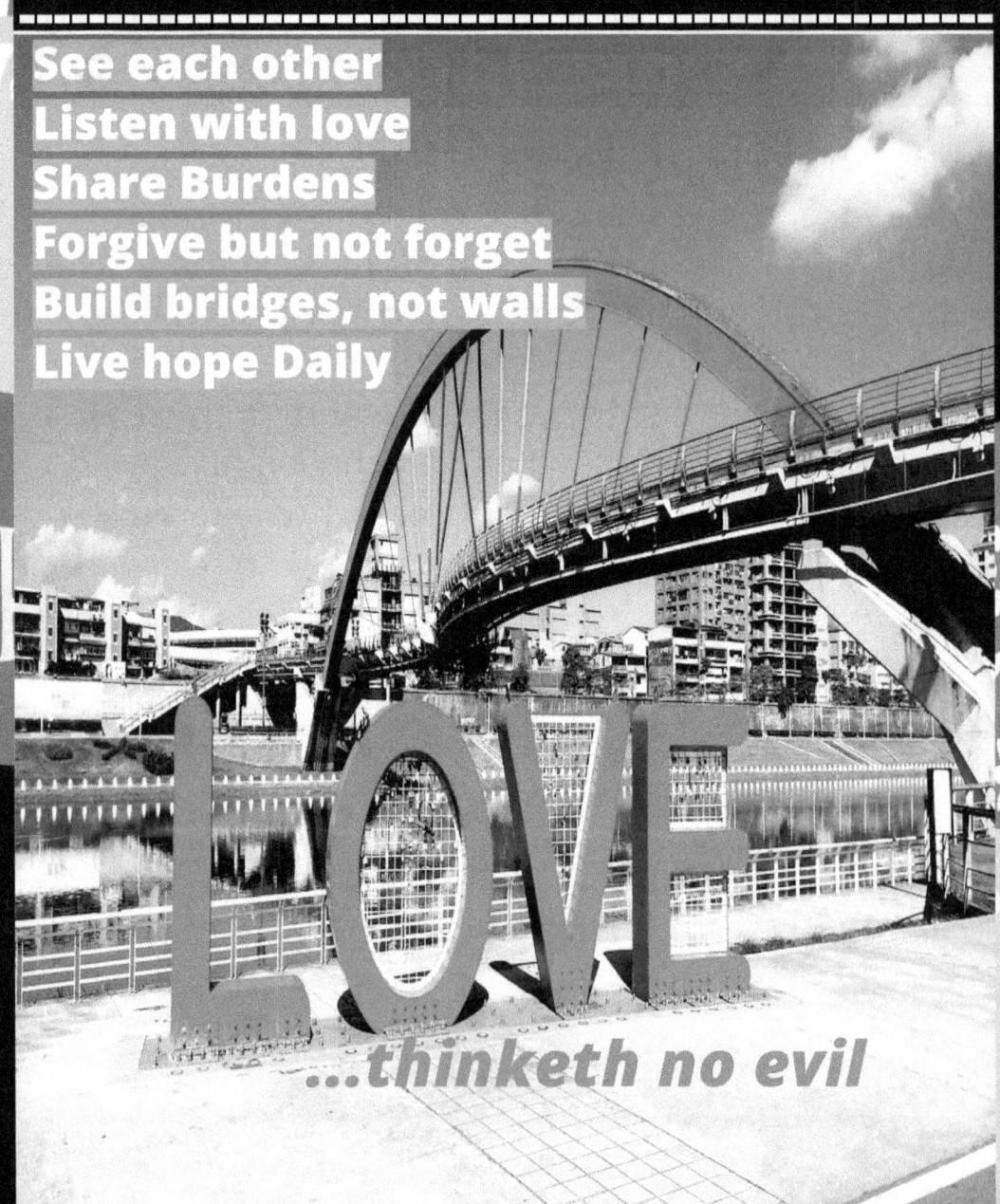

Love is the Bridge

See each other
Listen with love
Share Burdens
Forgive but not forget
Build bridges, not walls
Live hope Daily

LOVE

...thinketh no evil

An American Journey
Through Fire and Hope

LOVE IS THE BRIDGE

An American Journey Through Fire and Hope

Love is the Bridge

Part Three

Table of Contents

An American Journey Through Fire and Hope

Love is the Bridge

A New Fire

❄ Chapter Thirteen – A New Fire

The 2020s arrived not with a whisper, but with a roar.

A pandemic swept the world, turning neighbors into strangers behind masks. Streets emptied, schools closed, and fear spread faster than the sickness itself. Arthur watched from his porch as ambulances screamed down the street night after night.

Then came the protests — millions pouring into the streets, demanding justice after yet another Black life was stolen. He watched the footage with weary eyes: tear gas, shields, raised fists, chants echoing into the night. It was the sixties all over again, only this time broadcast in real time on every phone, every screen.

Sitting with his grandchildren one evening, he sighed. "The disease of hate has never died. It just mutates."

An American Journey
Through Fire and Hope

A New Fire

His grandson looked up at him, wide-eyed. "Then what's the cure, Grandpa?"

Arthur's heart ached at the question. He had spent a lifetime searching for that answer. He thought of his grandmother's words, of Lillian's last breath, of the students who asked how to carry hope. He knew the answer, though it was not an easy one.

"The cure is love," he said softly. "But not the kind of love that's just words. Love that listens. Love that sacrifices. Love that builds bridges when walls are easier."

Still, even as he spoke, he felt the fire of frustration. He saw division deepen like a canyon — families torn apart by politics, friends turned strangers by arguments online. Even churches split down the middle, unable to pray together without fighting.

Love is the Bridge

A New Fire

One night, on the news, he watched footage of men storming the Capitol, flags waving in anger. His stomach turned. "We are tearing ourselves apart," he whispered.

Yet amid the fire, he also saw sparks of something else. Young people delivering food to neighbors during the lockdown. Strangers linking arms in protests, protecting each other from harm. Teachers teaching over flickering video screens, refusing to let children be abandoned.

The fire of hate was raging, yes. But so was the fire of love.

Arthur realized then: every generation faces its fire. His had been hoses and dogs. His children's had been barriers and quiet prejudice. His grandchildren's was polarization, fear, and mistrust.

An American Journey Through Fire and Hope

Love is the Bridge

A New Fire

But in every fire, there had always been voices — voices refusing to let hate have the last word.

Arthur prayed that his would still be one of them.

✳ Chapter Fourteen – Still Standing

By 2023, Arthur McMillian was seventy years old. His hair had gone silver, his steps slowed, and he leaned more on his cane than he liked to admit. But his eyes — those steady, watchful eyes — had lost none of their fire.

He still went to the corner store every morning for the paper and a cup of coffee. And still, sometimes, the cashier asked for extra ID, studying his face a beat too long. Still, he felt the sting of being followed down aisles, of strangers assuming age and color meant ignorance.

One afternoon, while waiting for a prescription at the pharmacy, a young clerk spoke too slowly, too loudly, as if Arthur couldn't understand. "Sir, do... you... need... help filling this form?"

An American Journey Through Fire and Hope

Love is the Bridge

Still Standing

Arthur chuckled softly. "Son, I've been filling out forms longer than you've been breathing."

The boy flushed red, muttered something, and walked away. Arthur sighed. After seven decades, some things hadn't changed at all.

At a town meeting that year, he stood to speak about funding a youth program. A man in the back whispered, just loud enough: "Here comes the old Black preacher again."

The words burned, but Arthur did not flinch. He gripped the podium, leaned into the microphone, and spoke anyway.

"You can call me old, you can call me Black, you can call me whatever makes your tongue feel strong. But I am still here. And I will still speak. Because silence is the one thing I will not give you."

An American Journey Through Fire and Hope

Still Standing

Applause erupted. The whisperer shrank into his seat.

Later that night, his granddaughter climbed onto his lap. "Grandpa, aren't you tired?" she asked.

"Yes, baby," he said, brushing her hair back. "I am tired. But being tired isn't the same as being finished."

He kissed her forehead. "As long as I've got breath, I'll stand. Even if all I can do is stand."

Love is the Bridge

ARTHUR McMILLIAN

LOVE

...does not rejoice in iniquity

An American Journey Through Fire and Hope

❄ Chapter Fifteen – What Love Looks Like

Arthur had seen hate in every decade of his life. It wore uniforms in the sixties, badges in the nineties, and angry slogans in the 2020s. Hate was nothing new.

But what had carried him wasn't hate at all. It was love.

He thought of his mother, who scrubbed floors with cracked hands but still saved a dollar from every paycheck so he could buy books. That was love.

He thought of Mrs. Parker, the white teacher who slipped him novels in secret, risking her own career so his mind could be free. That was love.

He thought of Lillian, who gave him children,

Love is the Bridge

laughter, and courage, who reminded him with her last breath to carry love, not bitterness. That was love.

He thought of his grandmother, who told him hatred was heavy, love was lighter — words that had held him up through every storm. That was love.

He thought of Marcus and Renee, who grew into the very future he once dreamed of, who carried forward the lessons he feared the world would bury. That was love.

He thought of strangers too — the neighbor who shielded him the night of the beating, the students who called him Grandpa Arthur, the young activist who handed him a microphone when he thought his voice was gone. That was love.

Love was not soft. Love was not weak. Love

An American Journey Through Fire and Hope

What Love Looks Like

had teeth, courage, and endurance. Love was what showed up when hate thought it had won.

One evening in 2025, sitting on his porch, Arthur watched the sun dip low and thought: If only the world could see what I've seen. If only they knew what love looks like when it's lived out in the hardest places.

It wasn't grand speeches or perfect leaders. It wasn't laws passed or flags waved. Love was smaller, deeper, and stubborn. It was hands reaching across divides, forgiveness where none was deserved, kindness given with no promise of return.

That — he realized — was the prescription the world kept missing.

Not a theory. Not a slogan. But love in action. And if enough people lived it, maybe, just maybe, the world could be healed.

Love is the Bridge

See each other
Listen with love
Share Burdens
Forgive but not forget
Build bridges, not walls
Live hope Daily

LOVE
...rejoiceth in the truth

An American Journey
Through Fire and Hope

❋ Chapter Sixteen – The Prescription

By 2025, Arthur McMillian had lived seventy years in America's shadow and light. He had seen laws change, leaders rise and fall, marches turn into movements, movements fade into memory. And yet, one thing remained: the same sickness that had haunted his childhood still lingered in the air.

The disease of hate.

One evening, invited to speak at a local town hall, Arthur leaned on his cane and walked slowly to the podium. The crowd was a mix of faces — young and old, Black and white, hopeful and cynical. Some came to cheer him. Others came to scoff.

He cleared his throat, voice steady but low.

"I have lived through fire hoses, through dogs, through lies and fists and slurs. I have buried friends who never made it home from marches. I have felt hate pressed into my bones so deep it could have broken me."

An American Journey Through Fire and Hope

Love is the Bridge

The Prescription

He paused, eyes scanning the room. "But it didn't. Do you know why?"

Silence.

"Because I learned that hate is a sickness. And you don't cure sickness with more sickness. You cure it with something stronger."

He gripped the podium, his voice rising.

"The prescription for America, for this world, is simple — though living it is the hardest work of all.

See each other. Not color first. Not party. Not wealth. Just human beings.

Listen with love. Not listening to argue, but listening to understand.

Share burdens. No one carries freedom alone.

Forgive, but not forget. We cannot erase history, but we cannot be chained to it either.

An American Journey Through Fire and Hope

Love is the Bridge

The Prescription

Build bridges, not walls. Walls divide. Bridges carry us forward.

Live hope daily. Hope is not an idea. It's a practice. It's kindness in the grocery line. It's standing up when you see wrong. It's choosing light, even when night feels heavy."

He let the words hang in the air. Some nodded, some wept, some folded their arms. But all listened.

Finally, he leaned forward, voice soft.

"America doesn't need more hate dressed up as pride. The world doesn't need more fear wearing the mask of power. What we need is courage. The courage to love — not as a feeling, but as a choice. Daily. Stubbornly. Together."

He tapped his chest. "I am not asking you to agree on everything. I am asking you to refuse to let hate have the last word."

An American Journey Through Fire and Hope

Love is the Bridge

The Prescription

The hall fell into a hush, and for a long moment, Arthur simply stood, breathing, waiting. Then, slowly, a young woman in the back rose to her feet. Then another. And another. Until the room, one by one, stood in silence, not cheering, not clapping, just standing — as if bearing witness to a truth too heavy for noise.

Arthur closed his eyes, and for the first time in years, he felt light.

Because maybe — just maybe — the prescription had been heard.

An American Journey Through Fire and Hope

Love is the Bridge

The Light Beyond

Epilogue –The Light Beyond

The porch creaked beneath the weight of time. Arthur McMillian sat in his old wooden chair, cane leaning against the rail, the evening sun laying gold across his face. His grandchildren played in the yard, laughter ringing like bells.

He watched them with a tenderness that softened the deep lines etched into his skin. They were free in a way he had not been as a boy. No "Whites Only" signs. No hoses chasing them off the street. Yet he knew the shadows still lingered — suspicion, division, fear. The disease of hate had not died. But neither had love.

His youngest granddaughter climbed onto his lap, her curls brushing his chin. "Grandpa," she asked, "did you win?"

The question pierced him. He thought of Birmingham's fire hoses, of Dr. King's voice

An American Journey
Through Fire and Hope

Love is the Bridge

The Light Beyond

silenced too soon, of the blows he had endured, of Lillian's hand slipping from his own. He thought of every wall still standing, every bridge not yet built.

But then he looked into her eyes — bright, curious, unafraid. He heard the laughter of her cousins chasing fireflies. He felt the warmth of generations carried forward in their small hands.

He smiled. "If love is still alive in you," he said softly, "then yes, baby. I won. And so can we all."

The child wrapped her arms around his neck, and Arthur closed his eyes. For a moment, the years fell away — the weight, the sorrow, the fight. All that remained was light.

And in that light, Arthur McMillian knew: his journey was not the end of the story. It was only the beginning of theirs.

An American Journey Through Fire and Hope

Back Matter

Love is the Bridge

Acknowledgment

This book is stitched from many threads — the voices of ancestors, the courage of teachers, the wisdom of elders, and the hope of young people.

To my amazing brother and sister-in-law, Larry and Janice: thank you for your endless friendship and care. You are always there for me. You listen as I delve deeply into discussions about humanity, history, God's majesty, supernatural miracles, and healings.

To the men and women who lived through the Civil Rights era, who marched, who prayed, who suffered, who forgave — this story belongs to you.

To the students, activists, and community leaders who still build bridges every day: may your fire never be dimmed.

And finally, to the readers holding this book in your hands: thank you for listening, for reflecting, and for daring to believe that love can carry us further than hate ever will.

An American Journey Through Fire and Hope

Love is the Bridge

Arthur McMillian makes a vow at age thirteen to fight with dignity and love. How does this vow shape his choices across the decades?

Which character (Arthur, his mother, Mrs. Parker, Lillian, his children) left the deepest impression on you? Why?

The story suggests that every generation faces its own "fire." What is the fire of today's generation? How is it similar to, or different from, the struggles of Arthur's youth?

Forgiveness is central to Arthur's journey. Do you agree with his approach? Is forgiveness always necessary for healing?

Arthur says: "Love is not weakness. It is the hardest thing in the world." What does that mean to you personally?

What bridges do you feel need to be built in America (or your community) today? How might you play a role in building them?

An American Journey Through Fire and Hope

Love is the Bridge

About the Author

Mrs. Brown, affectionately known as "The Encourager," is a gifted storyteller and a member of the Lunch Box Puzzle Therapy Quick Relief Magnet team. She is also the creator and advocate of inspiring books that promote reflection and resilience. Through her *Mood of America Series* and *Joy of Being Series*, she skillfully blends narrative, history, and interactive activities, encouraging readers to think critically and engage actively.

In 2025 and beyond, Mrs. Brown aims to be a bridge and a voice by writing uplifting narratives that can make a difference during challenging times. She invites you to become a bridge in your own community. Ask yourself, "What can I do?" She encourages you to take action and do what you do best. Don't look back and wish you had acted; now is the time to step forward. Love your neighbor. Help your neighbor. Go out of your way to assist someone different from you. You were born to be a blessing, so be a blessing. It's your time to shine. Share your gift with others. You are the gift, the bridge, and the voice.

An American Journey Through Fire and Hope

Love is the Bridge

An American Journey Through Fire and Hope

Love is the Bridge

Catalog Offers

🗂 Mood in America Series Bundle Description

Mood in America: A Reflective Journey Through Words, Pages, and Color

The Mood in America Series offers a unique three-part experience that blends reflection, creativity, and mindful relaxation. Each theme — from Love is the Bridge to Healing Our Nation — comes alive through three companion formats:

🧩 Puzzle Book – Word search puzzles filled with meaningful words that spark thought, memory, and conversation.

📖 Guided Journal – Daily prompts, reflection pages, and inspirational quotes to guide self-discovery and mindfulness.

🎨 Coloring Book – Black-and-white illustrations paired with short, uplifting statements to encourage calm and creativity.

Together, these books create a powerful toolkit for personal growth and reflection in 2025 and beyond. Whether you choose one title or collect the full set, each bundle provides an immersive journey into the challenges and hopes of our times.

****

See All Titles In The Amazon Store

An American Journey Through Fire and Hope

Love is the Bridge

- -

My American Dream Activity

The "American Dream" means something different to everyone. Please take a moment to write down your version of it in 2025 and beyond.

For me, the American Dream is...

_____

_____

_____

One step I can take toward it this year is...

_____

_____

_____

One way I can help others pursue it is...

_____

_____

_____

*"Strength is softer than stone,
but firmer than fear."*

An American Journey
Through Fire and Hope

Love is the Bridge

The Time Capsule Activity

Imagine you could write a message to the people of America 50 years from now. What would you want them to know about your hopes, fears, and dreams in 2025?

_____

_____

_____

_____

My message to the future is...

_____

_____

_____

_____

If they could read this message, what do you most hope they would learn?

_____

_____

"Love always leaves light behind."

An American Journey
Through Fire and Hope

Arthur McMillian

The words we hold inside us shape the stories we live. May your words carry you forward with strength, hope, and purpose.

Love is the Bridge

Write down five words that capture how you feel about America in 2025 and Beyond.

1. _____
2. _____
3. _____
4. _____
5. _____

Take a moment to reflect:
Why did you choose these words?
What do they mean to you?
How do they shape your vision of the future?

An American Journey
Through Fire and Hope

Love is the Bridge

With Gratitude
Thank You
Bridge Builders

Arthur's closing words:
"The prescription for America, for this world, is not complicated. It is love lived out — daily, quietly, persistently. Love that builds. Love that heals. Love that refuses to let hate have the last word. My story is just one man's path. But if each of us chooses love, then together, our story will be strong enough to heal a nation, and kind enough to light the world."

"Be the Bridge"

With gratitude to the elders who told the truth, the teachers who fed the mind, the nurses who mended more than bodies, and the young people who refuse to let hate speak last. Thank you to my early readers and community partners for your eyes, your hearts, and your courage.

An American Journey Through Fire and Hope

Love is the Bridge

Special Acknowledgment
My Precious Daughter, Evita Shardaa
My "Baby Bear"

From the depths of my heart, I dedicate this page to my beloved daughter, Evita Shardaa, affectionately known as "Baby Bear." You are the spark that rekindled my flame—the voice that reminded me of the power, purpose, and divine gifts placed within me.

You have spoken words over my life that mirrored heaven's truth:
"Mom, you are so gifted. You can speak on a stage, write words of hope, encouragement, and joy, and speak to the person who is grieving, filled with sorrow and disappointment. You can heal with your words, your voice, your spirit. Just being around you is filled with the presence of God."

Those words, your faith, and your unwavering love have carried me. You saw in me what I sometimes forgot to see in myself. You reminded me that my hands, my heart, and my words were meant to build, to teach, to heal, and to create.

An American Journey
Through Fire and Hope

Love is the Bridge

You celebrated the birth of The Lunch Box Puzzle Therapy Quick Relief Magnet as if it were your own, calling it "brilliant." You marveled at the Mood of America Series and The Joy of Being Series as extensions of my God-given DNA. You honored my years of teaching—guiding children of all abilities, inspiring educators, writing guidebooks, speaking in schools and universities, developing new methods of learning—and you called it "amazing."

You reminded me that every poem, every speech, every workshop, every prayer, every miracle I've witnessed was not in vain—but part of a divine tapestry God was weaving through my life. You said, "Momma Bear, you have healing in your hands and heart. I've seen it. I know it."

And so, my precious daughter, I thank you.
For pushing me.
For pleading with me.
For believing in me when I hesitated to show up.
For calling me to write, to speak, to create, and to shine.

An American Journey Through Fire and Hope

Love is the Bridge

Your love has been my mirror and my motivation—reflecting the gifts God entrusted to me. Because of you, I rise, I write, and I release my work into the world with joy and boldness.

You are, and always will be, the living testimony of my purpose made visible.

With all my love, gratitude, and eternal admiration —

Momma Bear 🐻 🤍

Baby Bear,
My Heart Thanks You.

An American Journey Through Fire and Hope